CW00796847

The Reindeer Games

Zander Dowie

Grosvenor House
Publishing Limited

All rights reserved
Copyright © Zander Dowie, 2023

The right of Zander Dowie to be identified as the author of this
work has been asserted in accordance with Section 78
of the Copyright, Designs and Patents Act 1988

The book cover is copyright to Zander Dowie

This book is published by
Grosvenor House Publishing Ltd
Link House
140 The Broadway, Tolworth, Surrey, KT6 7HT.
www.grosvenorhousepublishing.co.uk

This book is sold subject to the conditions that it shall not, by way of
trade or otherwise, be lent, resold, hired out or otherwise circulated
without the author's or publisher's prior consent in any form of
binding or cover other than that in which it is published and
without a similar condition including this condition being
imposed on the subsequent purchaser.

This book is a work of fiction. Any resemblance to
people or events, past or present, is purely coincidental.

A CIP record for this book
is available from the British Library

ISBN 978-1-80381-566-4

A huge thanks to my wife for her support
in writing this book.

I hope that all children reading this book
continue to believe in the magic of Christmas!

Contents

CHAPTER 1

A Nightmare Christmas Eve

It was a Christmas morning like no other. It was 6am in Christmas Town, the capital of the North Pole, and Santa Claus hadn't returned from delivering his presents. Something was wrong...

Josie, the Head Elf, was worried. Santa had never been back so late after delivering his presents and this was her 372nd Christmas!

At 6am on a normal Christmas morning, the annual celebration parade would be nearly finished, but today it hadn't even started! Hundreds of elves lined the streets waiting to see Santa and his two reindeer, Leo and Flora, returning from their trip. Once Santa arrived, the parade would start, and the fireworks would be lit. There would be booming bangers, retro rockets, and fiery fountains. Christmas music would play from the speakers at the top of the huge Christmas tree. The food stalls in the square would open and start selling candyfloss, toffee apples, ice cream, and cookies.

But the elves had to wait for Santa...

Just then, Josie's watch began to beep. Santa Claus had entered Christmas Town!

"Thank goodness, he's back!" said Josie. "Reggie, follow me!" Reggie was Josie's brother and Deputy Head Elf. They both rushed to the paddock to meet Santa and the reindeer. It was important that the reindeer got hot chocolate and a massage after their long journey.

Santa landed safely and climbed out of his sleigh, but Josie could tell that something was wrong. Santa was not his normal self. His usual smile and jolly attitude had been replaced with an angry glare.

"My office, now!" shouted Santa as he stormed off down the snowy path. He sounded serious, so they ran to Santa's office to hear what he had to say.

"Unfortunately, the time has come for a change. My reindeer have served me well for many years, but they are getting old and the world is changing. Their memory isn't what it used to be. We got lost thirty-seven times. At one point, I had to pop down and ask a friendly kangaroo for directions to Sydney! The population is growing, which means more presents to deliver. The reindeer aren't quick enough or strong enough to keep up. And don't even get me started on the rooftops! Satellite dishes are popping up everywhere. The skylights and solar panels are making it so slippery. I almost lost control of my sleigh in Berlin, and the bag of presents skidded right off the back in Rome! These reindeer just aren't cut out for it anymore. If we don't find another way to deliver presents, next Christmas will be cancelled!"

Santa continued his rant. "You have three days to come up with a clever idea to save Christmas, or I'm calling the whole thing off! I'm going for a quick round of golf with the Tooth Fairy to clear my head then I'm off to bed. Start the celebration parade without me!" He stormed out of his office, leaving Josie and Reggie open-mouthed, wondering how on earth they would be able to come up with a plan to save Christmas.

CHAPTER 2

The Big Idea

Santa stood in his office and looked out of the window at the frozen lake. The lake was home to most of the North Pole's wildlife and was Santa's favourite place. On the west side of the lake, Santa could see a family of polar bears chasing after each other. East of the lake was a snowy hill, filled with penguins snowboarding and sledding.

Santa heard a knock at the door, and he called out to Josie and Reggie to come in, ready for the most important meeting of their lives. If they didn't have any good ideas to deliver presents, Christmas would be cancelled!

"I hope you've come up with some good ideas for me. So, who's first?" asked a worried-looking Santa.

Reggie and Josie looked at each other, both hoping the other would speak first. After an awkward silence, Josie walked over to the whiteboard and took out a blue pen. Josie was famous for her love

of blue. She had blue hair, blue lipstick and wore blue clothes. She wrote "Helicopter" in big letters.

"Think about it, Santa. We have the best technology team on the planet. I'm sure they would be able to build a helicopter that would allow you to travel the world in one night. I've thought of a name too... the Clausocopter! We would paint it red and there could be a Santa hat on top of the main propeller. It would allow for vertical take-off, and it could land on any rooftop. We could even make it silent so it wouldn't wake up the children. The presents would hang from the Santa sack attached to the bottom of the helicopter. It would certainly be warmer and drier than your sleigh!" She nervously looked over at Santa, waiting to see what he would say.

"I like it... but where would I refuel on the journey? What if the weather conditions are bad and I can't see where I'm going? The reindeer could see through the fog and snow, and always got us to safety in bad storms. Plus, I just don't think it's magical enough. The image of Santa and his reindeer is special, and all the children recognise it. Thank you, Josie, it's on my maybe list, but hopefully we can come up with something better. Reggie, did you have any ideas?"

Reggie walked over to the whiteboard. He was dressed, as he always was, in a leather jacket and a band T-shirt. Reggie was a huge rock music fan. His favourite bands were the Arctic Foxes, the Snow Roses and the Rolling Snowballs. He had long black hair that came down to his chest and wore giant headphones around his neck.

"My idea is wings!" he said enthusiastically. "What if we could create jetpack-powered wings so that you could fly from house to house carrying a sack of presents? It would take up much less space than the sleigh and would be perfect for landing on rooftops. You would be able to travel very quickly and, most importantly, you would look super cool!" Reggie finished his speech and looked eagerly over to Santa.

"It's a good idea, Reggie. You've clearly put a lot of time and effort into this so thank you. It does sound fun. However, it's just not very practical. How could I carry all the presents for all the children? And jetpacks burn a lot of fuel very quickly. I don't want to be burning lots of fuel and releasing all those fumes into the atmosphere. Global warming is a real thing you know. It's important we look after our beautiful planet. If all the ice melted, we would lose our home at the North Pole! Do either of you have any more ideas?"

The room went quiet once again. After some deep thought, Reggie cautiously asked, "Why don't you just find some new reindeer to pull the sleigh?"

"I would love to, Reggie. But none of the North Pole reindeer are up to the job. They just aren't fast, strong or smart enough to complete the mission. Where would we find reindeer that would be up to the challenge?"

Reggie sighed. "Well, isn't it obvious? You need the best reindeer in the world for this job. What's your favourite thing to watch on TV, Santa?"

"The Olympics," Santa replied instantly. "I love watching people from all over the world coming together to compete in lots of different sports. But what does that have to do with reindeer?" Santa pulled a confused face.

Reggie stood up and made his way slowly back to the whiteboard. He started to write slowly, with his back to the rest of the room.

"What if you hosted a competition that would bring the best reindeer from all over the world to Christmas Town? You could run a series of events to find the fastest, strongest, and smartest reindeer. The winners would join you on your sleigh at Christmas. You could create your very own Olympics!" Reggie stepped away from the whiteboard and, written in large letters, were three words: The Reindeer Games.

Santa burst from his seat. He had a huge smile on his face, and he punched the air with his fist. "YES!" he shouted. "That is brilliant. Well done, Reggie! This is the best idea you've ever had. The Reindeer Games... I love it. If we can pull this off, we may have just saved Christmas! But how can we pull this off?" He looked over at Josie because she was the organised one.

Josie took the pen from Reggie and wrote "Action Plan" on the whiteboard and underlined it. Then she added:

1. Invite reindeer to the North Pole
2. Build a Reindeer Village
3. REINDEER GAMES!
4. Choose the BEST OF THE BEST!
5. Save Christmas!

"Sounds like a great plan!" said a very relieved Santa. "I think it's time for me to send out a radio message to the reindeer of the world on Antler FM."

"Good evening reindeer. This is Santa Claus speaking to you directly from Christmas Town at the North Pole. I have some exciting news! I am looking for special reindeer from around the world to guide my sleigh on Christmas Eve. I want to find the very best reindeer, who have skills and talents such as speed, strength, and intelligence. I am hosting a competition to identify the best of the best. But be warned, it won't be for the faint-hearted. It is my great honour to invite you to the very first Reindeer Games! The games will start on the first of December. If you wish to enter, you will need to respond via Antler FM. Have a safe journey and good luck with your training! Ho Ho Ho!"

Reindeer from all over the world began to hear the message. The Santos herd from Brazil and the Tanaka herd from Japan were amongst the first herds to arrange meetings to decide who would be their representative. The excitement from all of the herds was at an all-time high. Every reindeer on the planet wanted to be flying Santa's sleigh on Christmas Eve!

CHAPTER 3

Skye's Great Adventure

Over in Scotland, the MacDonald herd were buzzing about the Reindeer Games announcement. The MacDonald reindeer were the most famous herd in Britain and wore their purple and navy jackets proudly. Skye was one of the youngest deer, with white fur across her body and brown fur on her face, ears, and legs.

"Wow, just wow! Imagine being one of Santa's reindeer!" Skye shouted following Santa's announcement. She could feel the excitement rushing through her veins.

"Mum, mum! Will you be entering the Reindeer Games?" Skye would have loved to enter, but she was still too young. She could encourage her mum to join though!

Skye's mum Bonnie was the leader of the herd. She was kind, calm, and very clever.

"I can't just choose myself Skye, we will have to go to a vote," Bonnie explained. Bonnie invited each herd member to vote for the reindeer that they wanted to represent the MacDonald herd at the Reindeer Games. Bonnie won with eight-five per cent of the votes!

"I just know you are going to win the Reindeer Games and win a place on Santa's sleigh," said Skye, with a huge smile on her face.

"Thank you, Skye, but please don't get your hopes up! The best reindeer from all over the world will be there so the competition will be very tough."

Ten months later, the MacDonald herd set off on the long journey to Christmas Town. After a week of walking, they were nearly there. Blue, green, and purple lights danced across the night sky in front of them. Skye gasped with amazement—it was the Northern Lights!

As they approached Christmas Town, they saw two large gates ahead which swung open. Josie and Reggie were there to meet them.

"Welcome to Christmas Town! You must be tired after your long journey. Please follow Reggie to the Reindeer Village. If there's anything you

need, please let him know," said Josie with a warm smile.

Following Reggie through the gates, Skye looked around in amazement. On the left were rows of gingerbread houses offering delicious treats. Skye could smell candyfloss, cookies, and chocolate in the air. On the right was a big red post office. She could see the children's letters to Santa arriving in postbags on winged bicycles and being sorted into piles by important-looking elves. Straight ahead she could see the main square filled with elves in bright outfits. The orchestra was playing Christmas carols while the choir sang loudly. In the middle of the square was the biggest Christmas tree Skye had ever seen. It was covered in bright lights, baubles, and tinsel from top to bottom.

"Have you ever seen such a wonderful place?" Skye asked her mum. Bonnie smiled at Skye, happy that her daughter was enjoying herself.

They passed the main square and walked down a snowy path towards the lake. There were penguins and polar bear cubs chasing after each other and rolling around in the snow. The reindeer followed Josie past the lake towards the Reindeer Village. In the Village was the Reindeer Lodge where all the reindeer would sleep. Skye spotted the brightly coloured jackets of the different reindeer herds. She saw the famous red spots of the Tenaka herd from Japan. She could see the red, white and blue stars of the Millers from the USA and she noticed the green and white stripes of the Musas from Nigeria. These herds were famous amongst reindeer, and Skye was starstruck.

Skye headed outside the Lodge to review the giant chalk board to read the week's timetable:

Day	Event	Skill
Monday	North Pole Race	Endurance
Tuesday	Ice Cube Challenge	Problem-Solving
Wednesday	Strongdeer Competition	Strength
Thursday	Big Christmas Quiz	Intelligence
Friday	Roaming Rangers	Navigation
Saturday	Rooftop Hurdles	Agility
Sunday	Sprint Race	Speed

Sitting at a long table under the board were some official-looking elves registering each herd's competitors. Skye pulled Bonnie over to sign up.

"Name?" questioned the elf.

"Bonnie MacDonald."

The elf handed her an entrance pass. On it was written *Bonnie MacDonald. Competitor.* That was it. Bonnie had officially entered the first ever Reindeer Games. Skye beamed at her mum with pride. Tomorrow, the games would begin, and her mum was one hoof closer to pulling Santa's sleigh come Christmas Eve.

CHAPTER 4

The North Pole Race

After months of planning, the first day of the Reindeer Games had finally arrived! Santa walked out to the main square, passing hundreds of cheering elves and reindeer, and stopped in front of the huge Christmas tree.

"Good morning! I would like to welcome you all to the first ever Reindeer Games!" Santa had to take a step back as the crowd went wild, cheering and clapping.

"I can't wait to find out which two amazing reindeer will be flying my sleigh this Christmas Eve. Now, it's time to meet the competitors!"

One by one, the seven competing reindeer walked out of the crowd to meet Santa. Josie grabbed a large red megaphone and introduced the competitors to the crowd. Josie hated public speaking, so this was a big deal!

"Our first reindeer, wearing the blue and yellow jacket from Ukraine is Ana Koval! Following Ana, wearing a jacket covered in red, white, and blue crosses, is Ole Pedersen from Norway!" After each competitor was announced, there was a huge roar from the crowd.

"Up next, in the purple and navy jacket, it's Bonnie MacDonald from Scotland!" Skye cheered extra loudly for her mum. "From the USA, wearing the famous red, white and blue stars, it's Logan Miller! Next, we have Maria Santos from Brazil! Check out her lovely blue, green, and yellow jacket! Give a huge cheer for our next competitor, wearing his white jacket with red spots, it's Ren Tanaka from Japan! And finally, please give a warm welcome to our Nigerian competitor wearing the famous green and white stripes, it's Kofi Musa!"

Santa wished the seven reindeer good luck and then turned back to the cheering crowd. "Before we begin the first event, we need to officially start the games. Drumroll please..."

The drummers started to bang their drums. As the beat became faster and faster, Josie stepped forward holding a large red button. Santa turned to Josie and, with a cheeky wink, hit the red button hard. Suddenly the air was filled with rainbow confetti and streamers. Above the post office, a huge sign saying "Reindeer Games" unrolled to whoops and cheers from the crowd.

Josie grabbed the megaphone once again.

"The rules of the Reindeer Games are as follows... The reindeer that wins each event will be awarded two points. The reindeer that comes second will get one point. The two reindeer with the most points after all seven events will fly Santa's sleigh on Christmas Eve. Now, it's time for our first event, the North Pole Race! To deliver all the presents in one night, we need a reindeer with great endurance and incredible fitness! The race is simple. Starting from the main square, follow the racetrack around the North Pole and back to the start. The reindeer who gets back to the main square first wins. Good luck to all of you!"

The competitors took their places at the start line.

"Good luck everyone!" shouted Skye from the crowd. Bonnie turned and gave her daughter a wink.

Josie started the countdown. "Five... four... three... two... one... GO!" A loud klaxon screeched, and the race was on!

Leaving the main square, Kofi was in the lead, tightly followed by Maria in second place and Ole in third. They charged down the hill towards the frozen lake. The polar bears and penguins had stopped their usual games to watch the race. They cheered as the racers sped past them. Ole passed Maria to move into second place as they were passing the lake. They took a right turn and headed down towards the Airy Fairy Forest. They were joined by a group of Arctic fox-cubs who tried to keep up with them, but their little legs just weren't fast enough! Rainbow fairies lit up the muddy trail through the trees in the forest. They looked like stars, they were so bright.

Ren had started to catch up with the front three and he pushed harder to speed up.

The screen in the main square was showing the race to the crowd of excited elves and reindeer, all cheering for their favourites.

The racers left the Airy Fairy Forest and sped towards Iceberg Creek. The creek was north-west of

the wood and was the most difficult part of the course. The reindeer had to leap across the water from iceberg to iceberg, without falling in. Kofi reached the water first and jumped gracefully through the air to land safely on the first iceberg. Ole and Maria closely followed. Unfortunately, poor Ren wasn't so lucky! He jumped a little too soon and plunged into the ice-cold water below. He swam back to shore and pulled his shivering body out of the water. He knew that he could not catch up now and he was freezing cold. His nose was turning blue! The medical elves ran over to warm him up with a blanket and led him back to the Reindeer Village.

The remaining racers continued to leap across the glistening white icebergs. At the end of the creek, Kofi was still winning but Maria had overtaken Ole into second place. The racers flew past the Reindeer Lodge and dashed towards the finish line in the main square. Kofi felt his body beginning to tire, and he knew he had set off too fast. Maria zoomed past him to take the lead, swiftly followed by Ole. The cheering of the elves was getting louder and louder.

It was time for the final push. Maria's face grimaced with concentration. She was exhausted, but she couldn't give up now! As she entered the main square, she could see the finish line ahead. She could feel Ole just behind her and she knew that Logan wasn't far behind either.

For the crowd, it was too close to call. There were fifty metres left, forty, thirty, twenty... Maria and Ole were side by side. Ole stuck out his long neck and pushed his nose across the line, millimetres before Maria. Logan whizzed into third place. The crowd cheered and rushed over to congratulate the competitors.

Skye dashed up to Ole and Maria to congratulate them on a great race. She then headed over to the First Aid tent, where Ren was lying on a stretcher.

"Oh Ren, I'm so sorry you fell in. You were so good in the race! Are you feeling better?" Ren gave Skye a small, embarrassed smile. "Yes, thank you, I'm feeling fine. Nothing hurts apart from my pride!" Skye giggled. "Now, you better get back out to the main square and find your mum! She'll be worried!" Ren said. Skye left the tent and returned to the main square to join in the festivities.

After the first event, Ole had two points and Maria had one. Bonnie had finished in fourth place, and Skye was so proud of her.

CHAPTER 5

The Ice Cube Challenge

The next day, the crowd gathered in the main square again to watch the second event. Josie cleared her throat and her voice boomed out from the megaphone.

"Good morning, everyone! The winner of today's event must have strong problem-solving skills. These humans are unpredictable, and every Christmas Eve delivery is different. We need you to think on your feet and stay cool under pressure!"

Josie pointed to her right. Something very big was hidden under a huge red and gold sheet.

"I want you to help me count down!" Josie told the eager crowd.

"Five... four... three... two... one..." they shouted excitedly.

The sheet fell to the ground revealing a large glass cube. Inside the cube there was a screen on the back wall and a table at the front. On the table were four buttons. One red, one blue, one green, and one yellow. There was also a big computer keyboard with giant keys, suitable for reindeer hooves.

Josie continued to speak. "The aim of today's event is to complete a series of challenges in the quickest time. Two points to the winner, one for second place. Good luck!"

The first contender to the cube was Logan. He looked nervous as approached the table and stared at the screen. The screen then started to speak:

Complete these challenges, you have three,
Each correct answer produces a key!
Mistakes will add to your overall time,
Incorrect answers result in slime!

The screen lit up and a riddle appeared.

Counting down to Christmas from one to twenty-four, a tasty treat lies behind every door. What am I?

Logan sat back and looked up at the sky. This was a really tricky one. What has treats and doors at Christmas?

"My tasty treat is a carrot, but I don't think that's the answer!" Logan thought. He was watching the large clock on the side of the cube that was counting up his time—thirty seconds... forty-five seconds... fifty-seven seconds... "This is taking too long!" he sighed. Then, the answer came to him in a flash.

"I've got it! Doors and treats—it must be an advent calendar!" Logan shouted. He rushed to type his answer on the giant keyboard. Once he'd finished, a bell rang. He was right!

On the screen, a green circle flashed up and then disappeared quickly. Logan was confused, but the second challenge then appeared.

I have stripes of two colours and I look like a hook. You'll give me a lick, but I'm not something you cook. What am I?

"That's an easy one! One of my favourites, a candy cane!" Logan quickly typed in his answer and the bell rang. He was correct. This time, a blue circle flashed on the screen before the third challenge appeared.

There was a picture of Josie and Reggie on the screen.

Josie and Reggie were both born on Christmas Eve. When Josie was six years old, Reggie was half her age. If Josie turns one hundred years old this Christmas Eve, how old will Reggie be?

"I hate maths!" Logan groaned. He looked down at his hooves and said, "This would be so much easier with fingers!"

The crowd outside laughed, and Logan gave an embarrassed smile. He had forgotten they could see and hear him!

"Let's think about this. Reggie was half of Josie's age so if she turns one hundred, Reggie will be fifty. It must be fifty!" Logan rushed to type in fifty. This time, there was no bell sound, just a nasty horn! He was wrong and a bucket of smelly green slime dropped on top of him.

"Yuck, that's disgusting!" screamed Logan as the crowd laughed.

"Keep going Logan, you're doing great!" shouted Skye from the crowd.

Logan started to concentrate again as his time continued to rise. Then he had a lightbulb moment! His eyes opened wide!

"It's ninety-seven! Reggie will be ninety-seven! He will always be three years younger than Josie."

Logan typed in ninety-seven on the keyboard and was met with a ringing bell for a correct answer. A red circle appeared on the screen and then disappeared.

The robotic voice spoke again:

Almost there, no need to stress,
Just the coloured buttons to press.
Enter the code to release the key
Only then will you be free.

Logan squeezed his eyes shut to try and remember. There had been coloured circles flashing on the screen after each challenge! "What colours were they?" he questioned out loud.

He used his hooves to smash the buttons. First green, then blue, then red. Once he hit the final button another bell rang, and his timer stopped. The clock read seven minutes and thirty-six seconds.

A secret hatch opened under the table and inside was a key. Logan opened the door of the cube and was greeted with a huge cheer from the crowd. Would his time be quick enough to get a space on Santa's sleigh? He had to wait for the other competitors to complete the cube to find out.

One by one the other competitors took their place in the cube, until only Bonnie was left. She nervously headed towards the cube, peeking at the scoreboard on her way.

Reindeer	Time
Logan Wilson, USA	7 mins 36 secs
Ren Tanaka, Japan	8 mins 25 secs
Ana Koval, Ukraine	8 mins 46 secs
Kofi Musa, Nigeria	9 mins 11 secs
Maria Santos, Brazil	11 mins 26 secs
Ole Pedersen, Norway	11 mins 31 secs

It looked like Logan was the one to beat! Bonnie entered the cube.

A few minutes later, she had completed the first two challenges and was ten seconds faster than Logan.

The third challenge was hard! Bonnie found maths very difficult. She heard the dreaded horn twice as she gave two incorrect answers and two lots of smelly green slime landed on her head! Finally, Bonnie got the answer right and quickly put in the colour code.

Her key was released, and the clock stopped at eight minutes and twenty-two seconds. Bonnie's head dropped with disappointment; it just wasn't quick enough—Logan had won! Bonnie was so disappointed.

As she left the cube, the first reindeer she spotted was Skye. She came running up to her with a massive smile to congratulate her mum on such a good effort.

"Mum, you should be so proud of yourself!" Skye shouted gleefully. "You were really good, and you came second, that's one point for you!"

Instantly Bonnie felt better. Skye was right, she'd tried her best and that was something to feel good about. The other reindeer were all beginning to make their way back to the Reindeer Village to celebrate Logan's win. Skye ran after Logan to congratulate him on his success.

"Well done, Logan! You deserved to win today, you gave a great performance." Logan smiled and gave Skye a nod.

After two events, Ole and Logan both had two points and Maria and Bonnie both had one point. It was going to be a close competition!

CHAPTER 6

The Strongdeer Event

Bonnie headed back to the Reindeer Lodge to clean up after being covered with slime, so Skye decided to explore the Reindeer Village a bit more. She came across the Antler's Arms and could hear that there was a real party atmosphere inside. Reggie was on the DJ decks playing tunes from the Rolling Snowballs and Josie was in the middle of the dance floor performing the tinsel town bop.

Skye approached the bar and asked the elf for her favourite drink, a carrot and cucumber crush. Sitting at the end of the bar was a large, worried-looking reindeer. It was Maria Santos, the Brazilian competitor. Skye walked over to Maria to introduce herself.

"Hi, my name's Skye. Are you looking forward to the Strongdeer event tomorrow?" Skye questioned. If she wasn't, she should have been. Skye could see the huge muscles rippling beneath her fur.

"No, not really, it's making me feel a little sick."

"How come?" asked Skye, confused.

"This is definitely my strongest event, and all of my herd are expecting me to win it. If I don't win this event, I just don't see how I will win enough points to guide Santa's sleigh on Christmas Eve. It's too much pressure. I don't want to let anyone down!" said a sad-looking Maria.

"Have you been training?" Skye asked.

"Yes, of course. I've never trained so hard in my life! I've practically been living at the gym."

"Then there is nothing to worry about." Skye looked up at the larger reindeer and smiled sweetly. "You've prepared the best you can. All you can do is be the best version of yourself. If you can do that, I'm sure the rest of your herd will be proud of you. More importantly, you will be proud of yourself, no matter the result!"

Maria was stunned. This was a lot of wisdom from such a young reindeer. She beamed at Skye and felt as though a weight had been lifted from her shoulders.

"Thank you, Skye. I already feel so much better. You're right, I just need to go out there tomorrow and do my best."

Maria leant over to Skye and gave her a great big hug.

"I'm off to bed. It's important to get a good night's sleep ahead of the big day. Thanks again, Skye!" said Maria, and Skye noticed she had a spring in her step as she left the pub.

The next morning, Skye headed to the main square to take her place to watch the Strongdeer event. Josie gave a short introduction explaining that this competition would be won by the strongest reindeer, and then the competition started.

An hour later, there were only two reindeer left to compete. The scoreboard had Kofi in the lead so far. Up stepped Ren. When the announcer called his name out, he winked at the crowd and posed to show off his bulging muscles.

In the first challenge, Ren had to drag a sleigh full of presents and cross the finish line in the fastest time possible. Metre by metre, he hauled the incredibly heavy sleigh forward. You could see the grimace on his face. He began to sweat, but he wasn't slowing down. Crossing the finish line, he was ahead of Kofi, but not by much. Knowing he needed to be faster, he ran to the second challenge—weightlifting, his speciality!

On either end of a huge candy cane was a bucket of coal. The reindeer had to hold the candy cane on their shoulders and squat down twenty times. Ren was struggling now. The squats were really hurting his haunches, but he managed to keep up a steady pace.

Nothing was going to get in the way of his victory! After his final squat, Ren let out a roar and dropped the coals to the floor. "Come on!" he yelled at the top of his voice, pumping himself up for the last challenge of the event. His lead had extended to sixteen seconds!

The final challenge was to lift three very heavy balls of ice and place them on a high ledge. Ren picked up the lightest ball first. It weighed as much as a fully decorated Christmas tree. He had to kneel to get his hooves around the ball, as it was so wide. He counted down three... two... one and heaved the ball as quickly as he could onto the ledge. This was the toughest test so far. The balls were heavy and slippery, and not easy to grip with hooves! Ren moved to the second ball and, with a great effort, managed to place it on the ledge. By the time he got to the third ball, his lead had increased to a whopping twenty-seven seconds! He was going to win! He leaned down to grab the third and heaviest ball. This ball weighed the same as Santa! Again, he counted himself down from three. He shouted in pain as he lifted the ice ball. The ice scratched against his legs and was very painful. Taking deep breaths, he tightened his grip and managed to get the final ball onto the ledge.

He turned round to face the audience and punched his hooves up into the air. "Yes! YES!" he shouted, and the crowd roared back at him. He had a strong lead with only one reindeer left to compete.

"Please give a warm welcome to our final competitor, Maria Santos!" shouted Josie.

Maria walked to the start line looking confident and focussed. She took a deep breath and remembered the words that Skye had said to her. "All you can do is be the best version of yourself." The klaxon sounded and she was off. Sparks flew from the bottom of the sleigh she was pulling it so fast. In a flash, Maria had completed the first part of the challenge and had a good lead on Ren.

The second challenge proved to be more difficult. Maria hated squats and had hoped they wouldn't form part of the challenge. Slowly but surely, she got closer to twenty. Her shoulders were aching, her legs were cramping, and her lead was disappearing. With only a few squats remaining, she paused for a quick breath ahead of the last push. She gritted her teeth together and forced the last squat out with a huge effort, but it was very slow. Ren had the lead again, but only just.

Maria headed over to the ice balls. She put the first ball on the ledge so quickly, some of the elves missed it. The second one didn't take much longer. She knew that it all came down to the third ice ball. She needed this to be really quick if she was going to beat Ren. She bent down to grip the heaviest ball and took one final breath. She groaned as she put all her remaining energy into the lift. She heaved the ball up onto the ledge. Instantly, her body relaxed as she knew she couldn't have done any better. She had been the best version of herself, just like Skye said. She didn't even mind if she hadn't won, she was very proud of herself!

She looked up at the clock and saw that she was three seconds quicker than Ren! The crowd went wild in celebration. The rest of the Santos herd were samba dancing in celebration and the elves were jumping up and down with excitement. Maria's eyes searched over the jumping heads of the crowd and found Skye's beaming face. She gave her a wink and Skye's grin widened. Maria had won the two points she had hoped for. Ren took one point for finishing second.

Maria now had three points and was in the lead. Ole and Logan had two points each. Bonnie and Ren had one point each. It was a very close competition.

CHAPTER 7

The Big Christmas Quiz

After celebrating Maria's win, the elves swiftly went back to work. They had a tight schedule if they were going to be ready by Christmas. The Tidy-Up Committee got straight to clearing the square ready for the following day's event. They put up a large stage with seven stools opposite a desk with the quizmasters' seats behind it. This was the Big Christmas Quiz!

The quizmasters were Josie and Reggie. They surveyed their stage proudly. Reggie filled large cannons with confetti and balloons which would be released after the quiz. Josie was busy scribbling questions down in her blue book.

The next day, hundreds of elves and reindeer flooded the main square ready to watch the Big Christmas Quiz. Reggie was dancing on stage as music from the Snow Roses blasted out. Josie grabbed her large red megaphone to announce the day's event.

"Today is the Big Christmas Quiz!" The crowd cheered and whooped. "We are looking for a Christmas whiz to do the biz and smash this quiz!"

Skye was extra excited for today's event. She was ready to cheer her mum on with the loudest cheer she had ever done. Bonnie had spent the last few evenings reading and revising, so Skye hadn't seen much of her. She was eager to see her mum in action and was sure she would do an amazing job!

The seven competitors started to mount the stage and the crowd welcomed them with cheers and applause.

When Bonnie came out, Skye whooped so loudly, the elf next to her jumped right out of his boots! Interestingly, the competitors were all different shapes and sizes. Maria was a large reindeer with huge muscles under her fur. Logan was a lot shorter and thinner whereas Ana was tall with a very long neck and legs.

The rules were simple. Once a reindeer had answered two questions incorrectly, they were eliminated. The last remaining reindeer would win the event and take two points. The runner-up would take one point. Reggie hit a button and a spotlight focussed in on Logan.

"Logan, the first question is yours. Good luck! When building a snowman, what vegetable is typically used for a nose?" Josie asked.

"That is one of my favourites, a carrot!" said Logan confidently with a grin.

"Correct! Great start Logan!" shouted Josie, and the crowd clapped.

After nearly ten minutes of questions, none of the competitors had got a question wrong so the quizmasters moved to the harder questions.

"Ana, in the UK, what type of pie is typically left out for Santa on Christmas Eve?" Reggie asked.

Ana paused and thought long and hard. Did Santa eat pies?! She was struggling with this one!

"Is it apple pie?" said Ana hesitantly. She wasn't sure.

"I'm so sorry Ana, that's incorrect. It's mince pie. Next time you get a question incorrect, you will be eliminated from the quiz."

After another twenty-five minutes of questions, there were only two reindeer left in the quiz, Bonnie and Kofi. These two reindeer looked very different! Bonnie was short with broad shoulders. She had the same white patch of fur on her nose as Skye and dark brown fur everywhere else. Kofi, on the other hand, was very tall and skinny and had light brown fur. He had pale blue eyes and very long antlers, one slightly longer than the other. Both sat on stage nervously looking at the ground. They had both answered one question incorrectly. They knew that one wrong answer would mean they were eliminated out of the competition.

Josie looked at Bonnie and asked, "How many doors would you open on an advent calendar before Christmas Day arrives?"

"Christmas is on the 25th of December, so there must be twenty-four doors!" Bonnie proclaimed.

"Well done, Bonnie, correct again!" Josie said with a smile.

Reggie then cleared his throat and directed a question at Kofi.

"On Christmas Day, where might you find a joke?"

"Wow, that's tough," said Kofi. "Might it be inside a Christmas pudding? Humans are always hiding things there! Oh, maybe it's in a stocking with the presents? I know crackers have coloured hats inside and some mini screwdrivers, might they have jokes inside too? Oh dear, I will just have to guess one... My final answer is that jokes are found in a Christmas cracker!"

"I didn't think you were getting that one Kofi, but well done. That is the correct answer," Reggie exclaimed. This was too close to call. Both reindeer were equally matched, and both knew LOTS of facts about Christmas!

The tension was rising in the crowd. Lots of the elves were nervously biting their nails or twisting their ears. Skye almost couldn't bear to watch! She was sending her mum lots of positive vibes and good thoughts.

Josie looked at the next question and read, "Bonnie, what Christmas song begins with the line, 'You better watch out, you better not cry'?"

Bonnie's face lit up with a beaming smile.

"I was in the Antler's Arms a few nights ago and this song came on the jukebox." She began to sing, "You better watch out, you better not cry, you better not pout I'm telling you why, Santa Claus is coming to town! It's 'Santa Claus is Coming to Town'!"

There was no doubt about this one; she was correct! Josie nodded and the crowd clapped again. The rest of the MacDonald herd were jumping up and down. They could sense Bonnie getting closer to victory!

Reggie asked the next question. "Kofi, which plant with green prickly leaves and red berries is a traditional Christmas decoration?"

Kofi bit his lip. He wasn't sure. He could only think of mistletoe!

"I think it might be mistletoe," he said. "I know mistletoe has berries, but I'm not a hundred per cent sure if they're red!" He paused and then stated, "Mistletoe, final answer."

Reggie looked at Kofi and said, "I'm afraid that's the wrong answer. The correct answer is holly! Sorry, but this means you are eliminated out of the competition. Great effort though, you are one clever reindeer!" He then turned to the audience and proclaimed, "The winner of the Big Christmas Quiz is Bonnie!"

The crowd went wild. Skye was jumping up and down, smashing her hooves together. She was so proud of her mum. The cannons went off with a bang and confetti and balloons shot out across the stage. Reggie's lights started to flash and change colour, and the whole main square looked like a disco. Skye ran up onto the stage to hug her mum, who had tears of joy rolling down her cheeks. Bonnie had done it. She was the smartest reindeer and had won the two points. Kofi took the one point for finishing second.

After four events, Maria and Bonnie had three points and were in the lead. Ole and Logan both had two points. Ren and Kofi had one point. It was a very close competition!

CHAPTER 8

The Roaming Rangers

After the Big Christmas Quiz, Bonnie, Skye and the rest of the MacDonald herd headed over to the Antler's Arms to celebrate. They toasted Bonnie's success with a Highland eggnog while Reggie played the bagpipes to make them feel at home.

Watching the celebrations from the corner of the room were two old reindeer. One of them was grey, with long gnarled antlers and a scar across his right eye. The other had bright white fur and sapphire blue eyes. Skye knew instantly who these were. They were Leo and Flora, the reindeer that had been pulling Santa's sleigh for hundreds of years! She had heard stories about them from the elves, and some of the younger reindeer feared Leo because of his scar. Skye wasn't scared though. She could see kindness in his eyes and felt instantly drawn to him. She walked over to them and smiled.

"Hello Leo and Flora, my name is Skye. I'm Bonnie's daughter! How do you do?"

"Well, hello, Skye. I'm well, thank you. You must be one proud daughter this evening! I watched your mother today, and she did a fine job!" replied Flora.

"I am so proud. She did amazingly! I was wondering if you could tell me what it's like to be one of Santa's reindeer?" Skye asked.

Leo's face lit up. He couldn't help but smile when he thought of his adventures around the globe.

"What other job gives you the opportunity to make millions of children happy?"

Skye paused to have a think. *Maybe a candy maker or toy shop owner,* Skye thought, but then again, she had never delivered presents on Santa's sleigh.

"I've seen the pyramids in Egypt, the rainforests of the Amazon, and the Great Wall of China, which is my personal favourite! It was the greatest honour of my life to pull Santa's sleigh."

Skye looked into Leo's eyes and could see a hint of sadness now.

"In truth, Skye, I am sad that I'm no longer useful to Santa. Christmas Eve was the most wonderful night of my life, every single year. Now I don't know what to do with myself." Leo looked down into his mug of mulled wine and sighed. Flora put her hoof around his shoulders.

"I'm also struggling to come to terms with the fact I will never guide Santa's sleigh again. It was such an honour and now I have no purpose anymore," said Flora, as a small tear dripped down her nose.

"You have so much to offer!" said Skye enthusiastically. "You might not be able to pull the sleigh anymore, but that doesn't mean you aren't useful! You have so many skills and talents, and a whole bunch of stories to tell! Why don't you use those talents and spread your stories to reindeer everywhere?!"

Leo looked into Skye's eyes and paused for a moment to think. She was right! He could already feel an idea coming to him.

"I know exactly what we should do now! Thank you, little Skye!" He finished his drink in one gulp and stood up from his seat. "Let's go Flora, I have an idea."

Flora hadn't seen Leo so excited for a long time. As he was turning to leave, Skye asked him, "What are you going to do?"

"You will have to wait and see, my friend!" With a wink, Leo and Flora left the pub with an extra bounce in their steps.

The next day, Josie stood in the main square to introduce the day's event. One of the key challenges Santa faced last Christmas was that he got lost several times. With the population growing and the rapid building of cities, it was getting harder to remember where everyone was, and the older reindeer weren't very good at following the SleighNav.

"The aim of today's event is to find a Ranger with good navigation and map-reading skills," announced Josie. "The one who completes the course in the quickest time will get two points and the runner-up will get one point."

Kofi from Nigeria was first to take on the course. On top of his green and white jacket was a bright blue sash, decorated with lots of badges. Each one was a different shape and demonstrated a particular skill. He was a long-standing member of Nigeria's Reindeer Scouts, and he wore his sash proudly. Josie passed him an envelope and issued the instructions.

"Don't open the envelope until the klaxon sounds. Inside, you will find a map which will direct you to the first checkpoint. From there, you are on your own. Good luck, Kofi!"

The klaxon erupted and the crowd let out a cheer. The Musa herd knew how good at navigation Kofi was and fully expected him to win. Kofi opened the envelope and could see a map of the North Pole. There was an X marked out near the frozen lake, which must be where he needed to head first. He began to run as fast as he could towards the lake. Once he reached the edge of the lake, he could see a wooden chest. He tried to open the chest, but it was locked and there was no key. He lifted the chest above his head and threw it to the floor, but it just landed with a thud and remained closed. It was clear the next clue was inside the chest, but he couldn't figure out how to open it.

"Come on Kofi, use your brain," he thought.

Written on the side of the box was *On the first day of Christmas my true love gave to me*. Kofi looked at the box with confusion, but responded out loud with "A partridge in a pear tree?" The lid of the chest popped open and inside was a telescope! He put it to his eye and looked around. When he looked across the lake, he could see a sign with an arrow pointing down to an X in the Airy Fairy Forest. He dropped the telescope to the ground and sprinted around the edge of the lake to the second checkpoint.

Under the sign stood three elves holding ropes and a harness. He looked up and could see ladders criss-crossing through the trees. The elves asked him if he was ready, and when he nodded, they began to fasten him into the harness and attach the ropes. They started to lift him up into the trees. As he was hoisted higher and higher, he gave a gulp. He was not the biggest fan of heights! He realised this was a slight issue for Santa's reindeer, so he was hoping that this challenge might help him overcome his fear.

Up in the trees, a trail of ladders was lit up by rainbow fairies.

As he started to walk, the ladders began to shake. He started swinging back and forth and his heart began to race. He was scared to move but determined to carry on. He continued to cross the ladders, one step at a time, not daring to look down at the ground. After what felt like an eternity, he could see a chest. Kofi gingerly reached the chest, legs still shaking, and read the lyrics on the side of it. *On the second day of Christmas my true love gave to me.* Kofi knew instantly what to do this time. He sang "Two turtle doves" out loud and the chest popped open. Inside was a compass and a scroll of paper. He flattened out the scroll and saw what looked like co-ordinates. Elves put Kofi back in a harness and lowered him to the ground so he could continue with the challenge. He was relieved to be back on the ground but did feel less scared of heights than before the challenge!

It looked like he needed to head north for two hundred metres, then east for fifty metres followed by north-east for twenty-five metres. With a grin, he hurried on, deeper into the forest. He wasn't worried about this part at all. He was fantastic at using a compass as he'd had lots of practice with the Scouts. He had a compass badge to prove it!

He ran to the final checkpoint without making any mistakes. In front of him was the final chest. The lyrics on the side of the chest read *On the third day of Christmas my true love gave to me.* Kofi quickly sang "Three French hens" and the chest popped open. Inside was an old silver stopwatch and a note saying "Time's up!" He immediately pressed the button on the watch to stop the time. An elf came to meet him and noted down the time from the watch.

"You can go back to the main square now, thank you!" stated the elf, and Kofi set off on the journey back to where he had started. Now all he had to do was wait for the other competitors and hope that his time was good enough.

With one reindeer left to go, Kofi still had the quickest time. The only reindeer that could prevent him from winning was Maria. He sat nervously waiting for her to return. When she finally did, she was shaking her head.

"I got east and west mixed up, so I went the wrong way!" she said sadly.

At that exact moment, the final times appeared on the screen in the main square, and Kofi had won by almost a whole minute! All his time spent earning his Reindeer Scout badges had been worth it.

In second place was Logan. With two events remaining, Maria, Bonnie, Kofi, and Logan had three points and were in the joint lead. Ole had two points and Ren had one point.

CHAPTER 9

The Rooftop Hurdles

Once the excitement of the Roaming Rangers had elapsed, the elves started to look forward to the Rooftop Hurdles the following day. The aim of the Rooftop Hurdles event was to find the most agile reindeer. Most of the elves believed that there would be a clear winner. Even the other competitors were worried because there was a famous ballerina amongst them! Ana, the Ukrainian competitor, was part of the famous Kyiv City Reindeer Ballet and had been the lead dancer in *The Nutcracker* five times. She was elegant and athletic and could jump so high—surely she would easily win this round?

There was a rumour floating around the main square that Ana was heading to the frozen lake to practise her ice-skating. A crowd of curious spectators made their way to the lake to watch, Skye amongst them. She stared in awe as Ana gracefully glided over the ice, effortlessly performing

a series of jumps and twists, giving her the illusion of flying.

At the end of the practice, Skye made her way over to Ana.

"Good evening, Ana, my name's Skye. I just wanted to say that your performance was beautiful. Your skating is so smooth and elegant. Where did you learn that?" questioned Skye.

"Hi, Skye. Thank you, you're very kind. My mother taught me to skate when I was young." Ana then looked at the ground.

"Are you okay, Ana?" asked Skye. After a few seconds of silence, Skye continued. "It's just an observation, but I noticed you didn't smile once when skating. You don't seem happy."

After another short silence, Ana looked up. "I've been training all my life to be a dancer on the stage and the ice. I just don't find it fun anymore. It's become more of a job than a hobby!"

"But you looked so free when you were skating. Those moves were awesome," Skye exclaimed.

"They are not my moves. I'm just practising what I've been taught by my coaches."

"Your coaches aren't here now. Why don't you just do the moves you want?"

"Because dancing without a routine is scary. What if I get it wrong?"

"If you dance without a routine, there is no right or wrong!" said Skye, smiling.

After another short silence, Skye asked Ana why she started dancing in the first place.

"Because I felt free when I danced. I had no limits and endless possibilities," Ana replied.

"How about you teach me to skate?" Skye asked, looking hopefully up at her.

Ana smiled at Skye. "Of course. Step forward onto the ice." Skye nervously placed her front hooves on to the ice and carefully began to walk forward. Ana showed Skye where to place her hooves. "Slide your left hooves first, then your right. Try and keep a nice steady rhythm and let your hooves glide across the ice." Skye began to slip and then she tripped over and crashed down on the ice. Ana helped pick her up. "We all fall sometimes. The main thing is to get back up and keep trying." Skye looked forward and began to set off again. This time, she felt more comfortable, and her confidence started to grow. She started to pick up speed, gracefully gliding side to side. Ana was really impressed and started to clap her hooves together in applause. Watching Skye skate so freely reminded her of her childhood and why she started skating in the first place, which filled her heart with joy.

As they came off the ice, Skye thanked Ana for her help and wished her luck for the event.

The next morning, Josie explained to the crowd of elves and reindeer that they needed to find reindeer who were very agile and would be able to avoid the many obstacles found on rooftops. As usual, two points would go to the reindeer with the quickest time and one point would go to the runner-up.

Ana was the last reindeer to take part. Ole currently had the lead, and by quite a long way. Ana headed to the start line and awaited the klaxon. A long, narrow house with a roof on top of it had been put up in the main square. The first part of the event required Ana to get to the other end of the rooftop as quickly as possible while avoiding all of the obstacles. If she touched any of the obstacles, ten seconds would be added to her time. Before she started, she looked over at Skye on the sidelines and smiled. On the klaxon, she set off across the rooftop. There were chimneys of all shapes and sizes, delicate shiny solar panels and huge round satellite dishes scattered all over. Ana moved quickly from side to side to avoid touching anything. Black ice and snow covered the surface making it very slippery and difficult for her hooves to get good grip. There were elves based either side of her, throwing snowballs to test whether the competitors could dodge them.

Luckily, Ana had learned to be light on her feet and was very good at twisting, turning, and jumping from all her years in the ballet. As she approached the end of the roof, she saw that she was going to have to climb down a chimney to get back to the ground!

Once she landed safely in the fireplace, an elf handed her a Christmas present wrapped in shiny blue paper with a large red bow on it. On top of the present was a note. It said: *Place the present under the Christmas tree without setting off the alarm. Every alarm will result in ten seconds being added to your time.* There were red laser beams criss-crossing the room between her and the beautifully decorated Christmas tree at the other end. She took a deep breath and made her first step forward. With the present gripped tightly between her front hooves, Ana began to dip and dive through the tangle of lasers, careful not to touch any. Halfway across the room, the lasers began to move up, down, left, and right, making it even harder to avoid them! She dropped down to her chest and rolled beneath one of the lasers. Then, quick as a flash, she jumped up to her hind legs and pirouetted over the next one, as if it were a skipping rope. Ana felt so free and invincible! She could see how close she was to the finish, but two lasers remained. Ana jumped into a diving forward roll and successfully missed the red lasers. She gracefully placed the unharmed present under the tree, and the red lasers disappeared. She had done it!

The crowd outside erupted into applause. It was a faultless run. Ana was the only contestant not to hit any obstacles or set off the alarms from any of the red lasers. Not only that, but she was also the fastest by nearly two whole minutes! As she left the room, she could see her name at the top of the leaderboard, and her eyes glistened with tears of joy. Ana looked over at Skye and beamed at her. Skye responded with an equally large smile.

With only one event remaining, Maria, Bonnie, Kofi, Logan and Ole had three points and were in the joint lead. Ana had two points and Ren had one point.

CHAPTER 10

The Sprint Race

After Ana's victory, Skye headed back to the Reindeer Village with Bonnie and the rest of the MacDonald herd. As they passed Antler's Gym, she noticed a new sign had been pinned onto the door. In big black letters, it said:

LeO aNd FloRA's LEsSoNS TODay. cOMe aND leARn abOUt SANta'S SLeiGH

Skye ran over to the window to peer in. She could see Leo standing next to a large blackboard, carefully drawing a diagram of Santa's sleigh. In front of Leo were two rows of young reindeer calves, looking up at him and listening intently. Flora was standing to one side, writing on a clipboard.

Had they decided to become teachers? Leo seemed to be loving it! His smiling face looked years younger than the last time Skye had seen him, and he was speaking animatedly to the young calves. He glanced up and caught Skye's eye through the window. He beckoned to her with one of his hooves, and shouted, "Come in, Skye, please come in!"

After a slight hesitation, Skye stepped nervously forward to the front of the classroom.

"Look here, young'uns, we have a visitor. Please can you all give Skye a reindeer welcome to our classroom." The calves all started to stamp their hooves on the wooden floor and whooped and cheered. Skye smiled self-consciously and gave a little wave.

"You don't know this, young'uns, but the reason Flora and I are here today is because of Skye. We were feeling very low, and Skye kindly reminded us that we all have skills and talents, even if we are old and feeling useless. I decided then that it was important for us to use the skills and knowledge we gained from working on Santa's sleigh to help teach people. This is why we decided to open our classroom." Leo said passionately. He then turned to Skye and declared, "Skye, you are welcome here any time. Please make sure you come to visit."

"I'd love to!" Skye exclaimed. She said goodbye to Leo, Flora, and the calves, and left the classroom with a huge swell of pride in her chest and a feeling of happiness for them. She made her way back to the Reindeer Lodge for a good night's sleep.

The following day, Josie made her last trip to the main square to address the onlooking elves and reindeer for the final challenge of the Reindeer Games.

"Good morning, Christmas Town!" shouted Josie, her voice booming into the megaphone. Each day she had been getting more and more confident, and today she sounded like a pop star greeting her fans on stage at a concert. "Thank you so much for joining me! What a brilliant week it's been so far. Gimme a cheer if you have been enjoying the Reindeer Games!"

The crowd erupted with cheers. They loved it! Josie was pumped and continued to shout excitedly into the megaphone.

"Now give me a *whoop whoop*!" She was thrilled to hear the crowd respond by whoop-whooping loudly. "How about a *boom boom*?" she tried. Once again, the crowd boom-boomed back at her. "Can I get a *zig-a-zig-a*?" Josie was in her element and the power was going to her head! As the crowd were zig-a-zigging, Reggie approached Josie and coughed loudly in her ear.

"Do you think we could get on with the competition at some point today?" he said sarcastically.

Josie looked at him sheepishly and then went back to announcing the event. "Today's one-kilometre sprint is all about speed. There are no secret loopholes to find, and no clever tactics can help you! It is simple— the fastest reindeer wins! It is really close at the top of the leaderboard so the two points for a win, and one point for second could be crucial."

For many reindeer, this was the biggest event. Everyone thought they were the fastest. They all wanted to brag about their speed! The seven competing reindeer headed to the start line. Reggie held up the klaxon, paused for a second and then squeezed it firmly.

In a flash, they were off. Kofi started off quickest and was in front for the first hundred metres. Bonnie and Ren also made strong starts and were very close behind him. The supporting reindeer herds were all waving flags of their herd's colours and cheering on their favourites. Ana had started slowly to save energy. Suddenly, she sped up and by the halfway mark, she was level with Kofi! Kofi was grinding his teeth together as he powerfully drove on, aware that Ana and Ren were hot on his heels. Ana's face was scrunched up with concentration as she pushed on, harder and harder. Ren continued to make ground until he was neck and neck with Kofi and Ana as the finish line was rapidly approaching. Ren was currently the only reindeer who hadn't won an event. He could hear his herd shouting encouragement from the sidelines and was determined to give everything to win this race. They crossed the finish line at what seemed like the same time. Not even the judges could tell who was first.

"We are going to have to rewind the DeerCam to see who has won! This is too close to call!" Josie announced, and a hush swept through the crowd.

Everyone was staring up at the big screen to watch the slow-motion replay. The crowd watched on in silence as the replay began. By the width of an antler, Ren had won the race, closely followed by a nose length from Ana with Kofi in third! Ren had secured the two points, Ana had won one point.

The Japanese herd burst into celebration! They ran onto the racetrack and picked up Ren, carrying him around the track. They were incredibly proud of him.

While Ren was celebrating, Santa made his way to the main square for the medal ceremony. He picked up the megaphone and waited for the excited crowd to fall silent.

"On Christmas morning last year, I feared that I would no longer be able to deliver presents, and that the magic of Christmas would be lost. I am pleased to say that I am no longer concerned!"

The crowd of elves and reindeer started to jump with joy.

"I have been blown away by the competitors I have seen this week, and it was a joy to witness every single one of you trying your best. Now, for the moment we've all been waiting for! The two reindeer with the highest points, and guiding my sleigh are…

it's a tie!" All seven reindeer had accumulated three points! The elves began to whisper to each other. *What happens now? Is there a tie-breaker? How will Santa decide who the winners are?*

Santa called Josie and Reggie over and they began to talk in a huddle. After what felt like an eternity, Santa stepped forward and lifted up the megaphone. "I need reindeer on my sleigh with the right characteristics to help me successfully deliver presents to children all over the world. All seven reindeer demonstrated unique abilities that will be very useful for me come Christmas Eve. Therefore, I am delighted to announce that all seven reindeer will guide my sleigh on Christmas Eve! So the first reindeer guiding my sleigh demonstrated great endurance. He was the winner of the North Pole Race, it's Ole Pedersen!" Ole looked stunned and began to walk forward towards Santa. Santa continued, "From now on, the winner of the North Pole Race will be known as Blitzen, because they are a force to be reckoned with." Blitzen leaned forward so Santa could put a gold medal around his neck. Santa gave him a magical blue jacket to wear that would allow him to fly.

Next up, Santa announced the winner of the Ice Cube Challenge and Logan made his way forward.

"You have shown excellent problem-solving skills. From this day forward, the winner of the Ice Cube Challenge will be known as Comet, because comets are extremely bright." Santa gave Comet his gold medal and a yellow jacket.

Santa then announced the third reindeer that would help guide his sleigh on Christmas Eve. The third reindeer was Maria, who had won the Strongdeer Event.

"Congratulations, Maria, you have shown phenomenal strength. From this day forward, the winner of the Strongdeer Event will be known as Donner, because they are the strongest and can defeat anything." Santa gave her an orange jacket to wear as well as her gold medal. The Santos herd started to dance in celebration.

Then came Bonnie who was the smartest reindeer after winning the Big Christmas Quiz. The smartest reindeer would now be called Vixen, due to their intelligence and wit. Santa gave her a medal and green jacket. Skye was bursting with pride and began to cry happy tears. This was the best day of her life.

Following Bonnie was the winning Ranger, Kofi. He made his way to Santa and collected his gold medal and white jacket. He would now be known as Prancer, because rangers use energy and determination to reach their target.

Santa then announced the winner of the Rooftop Race and welcomed Ana to step forward. Ana pirouetted towards Santa.

"Well done, Ana, your performance was breathtaking." He informed Ana that the winner of the Rooftop Race would be known as Dancer, due to their great agility and grace, and gave her a purple jacket and gold medal.

Finally, Santa asked Ren to come forward who had earlier won the Sprint Race. He gave Ren a red jacket and informed him that the champion of speed would be known as Dasher.

"Every one of these reindeer deserves a place on my sleigh. They all have unique skill sets that make them incredibly valuable to me. I would like you all to give a huge round of applause to my seven reindeer!" Santa requested. The crowd obliged and the noise was deafening!

Then Santa paused and, with a cheeky smile, said, "However, my sleigh is not quite complete. It is missing one key ingredient." The elves and reindeer looked confused. *Would there be another event? Who could it be?*

"I have come to realise that strength, stamina, and intelligence are important, but that there is another trait which is equally as important. Over the past week, I've had my eye on a very special reindeer. This reindeer has demonstrated love and compassion to everyone. They have shown kindness when others were sad and have been thoughtful and generous. They have displayed wonderful Christmas spirit and would be a great asset on my sleigh. Would you do me the honour of guiding my sleigh on Christmas Eve... Skye MacDonald?"

With a gasp, the audience all turned to look at Skye. Skye couldn't believe it. Had Santa really just called out her name? She stood there open-mouthed until one of the elves nudged her forwards.

"Go to Santa, go to Santa!" he said. Slowly, Skye made her way up to the stage until she came face to face with Santa.

"Are you sure about this?" questioned Skye. "I'm only small. And I didn't win any of the events!"

"You may be small Skye, but you have the biggest heart. From now on, the kindest reindeer will be known as Cupid, for showing love and compassion." Santa smiled as he gave her a gold medal and placed a pink jacket on her back. Her dream had come true.

The eight reindeer stood in front of Santa's sleigh as he used his magic to make a harness appear and clip them together. Skye proudly stood at the front with Bonnie next to her. Skye felt sure she was about to wake up from a dream, but this was real!

"I think it's time we go for a test drive!" shouted Santa and pulled the reins. "Dasher, Dancer, Prancer, and Vixen, Comet, Cupid, Donner, and Blitzen— let's GO!"

The reindeer charged forward until they had picked up enough speed to take off. As they rose to the starry sky above, Santa leaned over the side of his sleigh and called down to the crowd below,

"Ho Ho Ho! Merry Christmas everyone!"

Milton Keynes UK
Ingram Content Group UK Ltd.
UKHW052113171023
430787UK00010B/125